For Melanie, Inga, Kathrin, and Barbara, with love
– *M.R.*

For Keeley and Chloe – *J.C.*

Text copyright © 2005 by Marion Rose
Illustrations copyright © 2005 by Jason Cockcroft

Published by Bloomsbury Publishing, New York, London, and Berlin
Distributed to the trade by Holtzbrinck Publishers

Library of Congress Cataloging-in-Publication Data
Rose, Marion.
The Christmas tree fairy / written by Marion Rose ; illustrated by Jason Cockcroft.-1st U.S. ed.
p. cm.
Summary: Young Meredith loves her fairy wings more than anything, and when she helps the fairy at the top of her
family's Christmas tree, the sprite repays her by granting her deepest wish.
ISBN-10: 1-58234-668-2 o ISBN-13: 978-1-58234-668-7
[1.Christmas-Fiction. 2. Fairies-Fiction. 3. Wishes-Fiction.] I. Cockcroft, Jason, ill. II. Title
PZ7.R71753Chr 2005   [E]-dc22   2005045311

First U.S. Edition 2005
Printed in China
1 3 5 7 9 10 8 6 4 2

Bloomsbury Publishing, Children's Books, U.S.A.
175 Fifth Avenue, New York, NY 10010

THE CHRISTMAS TREE FAIRY

WRITTEN BY

MARION ROSE

ILLUSTRATED BY

JASON COCKCROFT

BLOOMSBURY
CHILDREN'S
BOOKS

M

Meredith MacCauley loved her old wings.

She wore them everywhere.
She wished one day she could fly,
just like a real fairy.

Then, one dark Christmas night,
Meredith heard a tiny cry.

"Help!"

Meredith tiptoed downstairs.
"Oh!" she gasped.
The Christmas tree fairy had fallen
from the top of the tree! She was
hanging off a very high branch.
"I've dropped my wand," the fairy
wailed. "I can't fly without it!"
Meredith looked around until she
saw it shining on the floor. "It's
here," she called.
"Send it back to me," cried the fairy.
"Wave it once and say
'Whizzery Swishery' twice.
That will make it fly!"

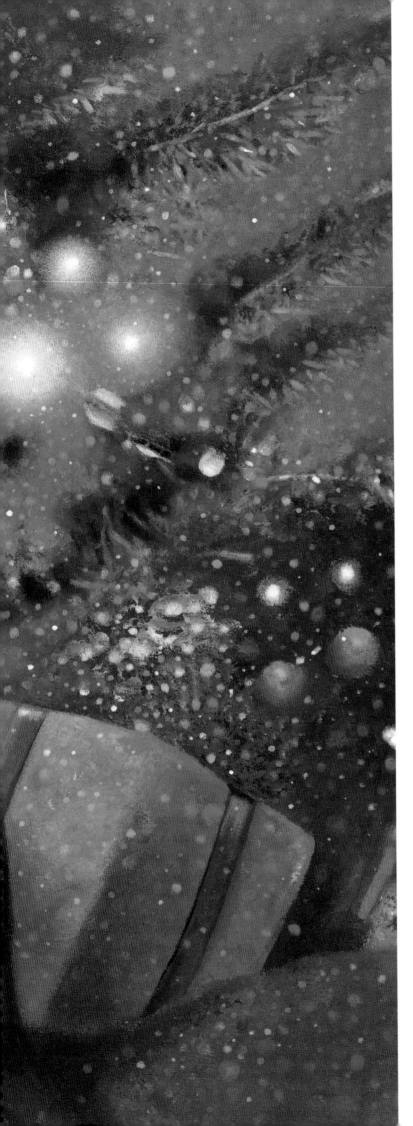

Meredith's heart fluttered like a butterfly. She waved the wand. "Whizzery Swishery! Whishery Swizzery!" she said. Oh no! Her tongue got in a twist. The spell came out all wrong.

Suddenly she was very small and the tree was very TALL.

"Spangle," groaned the fairy. "Whoops! Sorry!" whispered Meredith. "Just bring it up then," the fairy said, a bit bossily. "But hurry!" Meredith began to climb. It wasn't too hard. The branches made a ladder. And the wand lit the way. But suddenly . . .

"Is that the star?" asked the shepherd boy. "I've been waiting ages to see it."

"Um—no," Meredith said. "It's a wand."

"Ooh!" the boy sighed. "Where is the star? I do wish it would come."

Meredith thought.

"I'm going to the Christmas tree fairy," she said. "I'll tell her your wish, if you like."

"Oh, will you?" replied the shepherd boy, gazing at her. "Thank you! Hey, are you a real fairy?"

But Meredith was already
  climbing on . . .

and on . . .

The tree was dark and a bit scratchy. But it smelled nice, like minty chocolate.

Meredith passed a silver bell and then . . .

"Is that the sleigh?" asked the baby reindeer. "Did I hear it?"
"Um—no," Meredith said. "There's no sleigh yet."

The little reindeer burst into tears. "But why is it taking so long?" she sobbed. "I wish I could meet Santa's reindeer."

Meredith gave the reindeer a hug.

"There, there! I'll tell the Christmas tree fairy. I'm sure she'll help."

"Ooh!" the reindeer squealed. "You're going to make my wish come true!"

Meredith climbed higher . . .

and higher . . .

Her legs ached but she was getting near the top.
Suddenly—

BANG!

A strange creature stood in her way. She could smell its fiery breath.
"Ho! Ho! Ho! I am the cracker dragon!" it roared. "If you want to pass, you must answer my riddle." It twirled its whiskers fiercely.
Meredith trembled, but she had to go on and help the fairy.
"Ask me then," she said bravely.

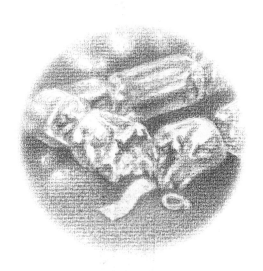

"What light shines most brightly when it is out?" the cracker dragon demanded.

There was a long silence.

Meredith tried to think.

The cracker dragon huffed and puffed while it waited.

"I don't know," Meredith said at last. "Tell me!"

But the cracker dragon just crumpled into a little heap.

"I can't," he groaned. "I don't know the answer. I lost it ages ago. Oh— how I wish I knew."

He looked so sad. Meredith patted his claw.

"The Christmas tree fairy will be able to help you, I'm sure," she whispered, "if you could just let me pass."

"Fairies? Wishes? Humbug!" the cracker dragon grumbled. But he moved his claw anyway.

So Meredith MacCauley hurried on.
At last, she reached the high branch.

She crawled all the way

along it to the fairy.

The fairy beamed at Meredith. She grabbed her wand.
Then she flew—all around the tree top!

Meredith watched her. The fairy was . . . beautiful! If only she,
Meredith MacCauley, could do THAT!

The fairy swooped down and sat beside Meredith.
"Now," she said, "what can I do for you? Three wishes, I expect."
"Gosh!" said Meredith MacCauley. So these things really did happen!

"Be careful what you ask for," the fairy warned. "It's three wishes and no more."
So Meredith thought very carefully about flying and all the other fantastic things she could ask for. Then she whispered in the fairy's ear.

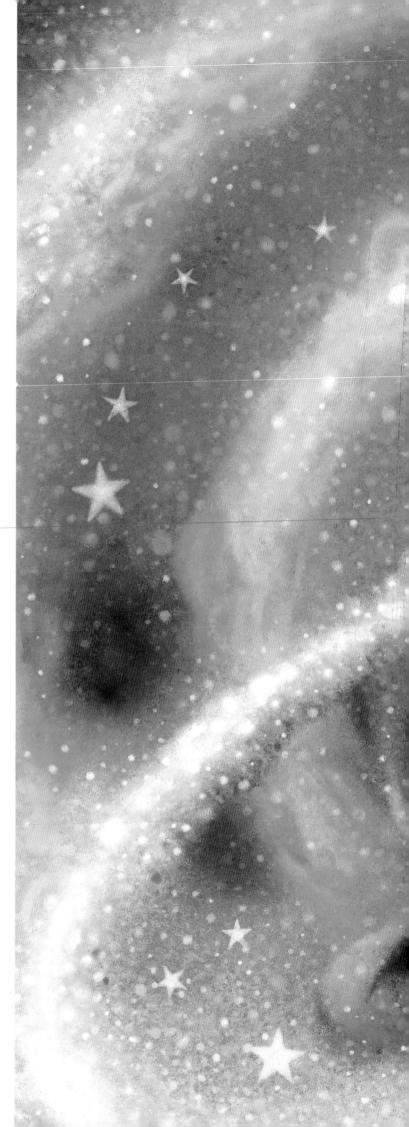

"Are you sure?" said the fairy.
Meredith nodded.
"You don't want to change your mind?" said the fairy.
Meredith shook her head.
"Well then," said the fairy, and she waved her wand.
And Meredith MacCauley's three wishes all came true.

"Oh!" breathed the shepherd boy,
gazing at the star.

"Look at me!" squeaked the baby
reindeer. "She made my
wish come true!"

"Ho! Ho! Ho!" the cracker dragon
roared again, this time at his own joke.
What light shines most brightly
when it is out? A star!

For a long, magical moment Meredith and the fairy sat together
and watched the night sky.
Then the fairy squeezed Meredith's hand. "Spangle," she said.
"Christmas is nearly here. I shall have to fly you back!"
She raised her wand at once and cried,

"Whizzery Swishery!

Whizzery Swishery!"

And then she, Meredith MacCauley, FLEW!

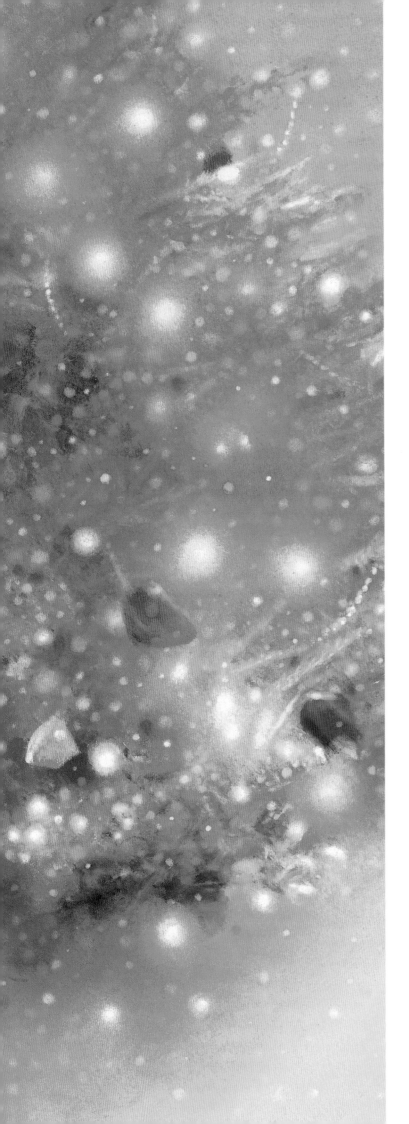

The next morning, there was another present under the tree.
Meredith tore it open.
"Ooh!" she breathed.

Meredith MacCauley loved her old wings, but these were even more perfect. She wore them everywhere. And she wished one dark, magical night that she could meet her fairy again.

To Meredith

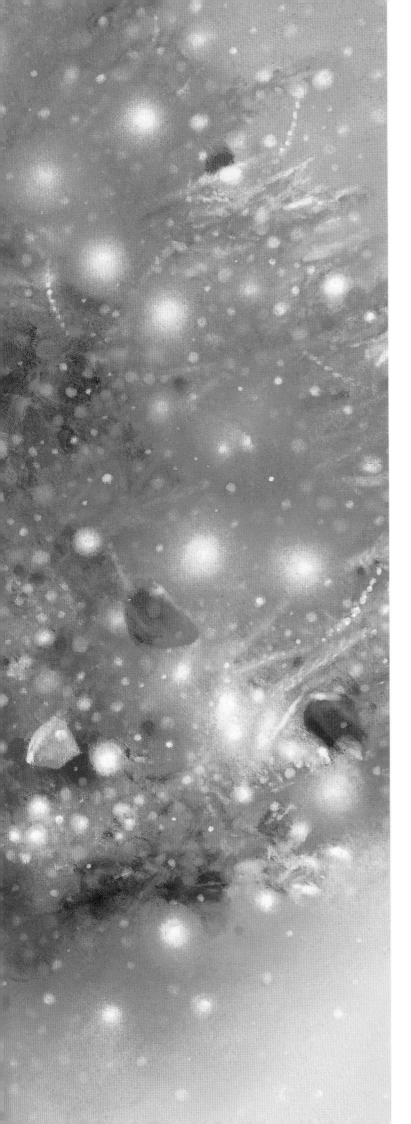

The next morning, there was another present under the tree.
Meredith tore it open.
"Ooh!" she breathed.

Meredith MacCauley loved her old wings, but these were even more perfect. She wore them everywhere. And she wished one dark, magical night that she could meet her fairy again.

To Meredith

And so did all the others!